Blood
Protectors
Collection

Sue Carpenter

Contents

	IV
1. ROSIE	1
2. SHAWNA	10
3. CASSIDY	29
4. JANICE	32
5. BETTY	38
6. DANA	64
7. GABBY	82
Acknowledgements	93
About the author	95

Being bitten is not always a bad thing.

ROSIE

Rosie

Everybody tries to make the most of their life, taking up opportunities, reaching for goals. This is even more so when your life has a span of only seven days. Buzzing around downtown Auckland, I'm focused on my goal of finding my Blood. For us mosquitoes, one human's Blood could enhance and prolong our lives, we just have to find that one. As a group of teenagers board a ferry, so do I. We haven't even left the wharf before I find her.

The ride isn't too long or rough to Rangitoto Island as I stow away inside the cabin. watching my Blood from a distance. If my wings get water on them, I won't be able to fly till they are dry again and could lose her. If lose her after seven days, I won't be able to transform and will not get to live a longer life. So long as I taste my Blood's blood every seven days, I live until she dies.

The school kids, teachers and parents jump off the ship, gathering their gear, and walk along a track to the next island over – Motutapu Island. Some girls have only been walking for ten minutes when they start complaining about the dust all around. I don't have an issue flying through dust, and my Blood is with a group of boys laughing. She chats the whole time without a worry or complaint.

They trot off over a quaint wooden bridge and up a steep hill where I'm amazed by the view over the Hauraki Gulf to Great Barrier Island and the Coromandel. When I transformed to her Blood Protector all her information was gifted to me, so like her, I know the names of the islands around us but when the teacher says we have 1000 meters to walk I have no idea if that's a long way or not.

One girl trips over as she falls down the steep hill, my Blood stops to help her. Thankfully I have a kind human Blood.

I observe her as she arrives at camp and settles in. They are put into groups, camp set up, and they start activities. Building a raft with barrels, which tips over and sinks to splashes and laughter, they all get wet. Most of the girls scream during all the activities, not my Blood. She laughs with her friends. When they are snorkelling, the leader opens a kina, causing lots of fish to swim around snacking. Then kayaking, and an obstacle course with a zip line where they lose focus, they fall in mud. The next day they climb pillars with a harness and have to do a star jump at the top, which most students don't do. She does. Orientation is the last activity before lunch. During the free time, the girl that had fallen over asks my Blood to go for a walk with her and they find a gun emplacement. The two girls sneak in to look and the girl who tripped over closes the door on her friend companion and runs off laughing. My Blood had helped her. I was about to change and open the door when three other girls appeared laughing.

'Help,' my Blood screams from inside.

Little shits, I leave and buzz off to get a teacher, but first I need clothes.

Ruby

Always my luck, every time I think a girl is nice, she flips. I wouldn't care if I wasn't claustrophobic. 'Let me out, please.' The space is getting smaller and darker by the second. I lie down at the crack by the bottom of the door, breathing in the fresh air. Aside from the ringing in my ears, I can hear cackling. Why won't they pick on someone else, just once? I had been having the time of my life. I push against the door and the hinge moves a little. I push with all my strength and it gives a little more. The hinges are rusted – perfect. I stand up and do a giant kick like my friend Danny had taught me. Pow! The door falls off and I climb out, covered in dirt from the ground.

The girls stop laughing as I charge at them.

'The mud monster's gonna get us,' one screeches.

I pick up more mud and charge at them, rubbing dirt and grass in the r hair and on their clothes, as I quickly catch up.

'Stop it!' Mrs Johnston calls.

'Enough!' shouts the school dean.

I grab dirt and throw it at them as Mr Dunlop, the headmaster picks me up and throws me over his shoulder. This doesn't stop me kicking and punching the air. 'Put me down Dad, I can hold my own.'

'I know. I am proud of you.'

'How did you know?'

'The girl in the white told us.' We looked where he pointed.

'What girl?' I ask looking at the teachers. There are only the two other teachers but there is a white dress on the ground. I run away from dad and charge towards the water to get clean.

'What happened?' Avi asks, diving in after me. 'Not telling yet,' I say.

'You're never calm.' Ian laughs diving in too.

'Wish I was a guy,' I say, 'then they wouldn't tease me.'

'They still would Ruby, you are the headmaster's kid.'

The mean girls come down to the water's edge dirty, the boys all laugh at them. As they dip their toes in the water, they scream saying it's too cold.

'Clean yourself, girls,' Dad says, so they all dunk under the surface, re-emerging clean as quick as possible and run off to the dorms. I know they will be putting something in my sleeping bag. Two of them are in my cabin group.

Rosie

I have almost been seen by my Blood, that's against the rules, I have to be more careful; I watch as the human toads put a frog in my Blood's sleeping bag, poor frog, but hey, it would eat me in my natural form if t got half a chance so as a human I find more and put them in all the mean girls sleeping bags. Transformed, I buzz into the corner watching over everyone. Whatever the girls try to do to Ruby, I save the day. Spaghetti, in Ruby's pillowcase, I cleaned it and put spaghetti in their pillowcases, unseen by all. I take the laces out of their shoes, as they do everything to ruin her trip, but fail each time. I love a challenge and being Ruby's Blood Protector is going to be fun.

They will never hurt her again.

SHAWNA

Sarah

My hand is up in the air, singing along at the top of my voice as the band's music shakes the valley full of partygoers. A week ago, I hadn't known the band, but have crammed listening to them all last week and learnt most of the lyrics. And the show is great.

It has been the wettest February in the history of forever, but the sun is finally out. My skin is getting pinker by the minute. Burning. Imagine if I hadn't put on sunscreen and a hat. I guess my skirt is too short like mum had said. With pink legs I won't be able to wear jeans for a week.

A mosquito lands on me. Electricity, as it bites, lingering. I am about to swat it when it flies over the crowd. My head fizzes like a shaken-up Fanta.

I pull away from my friends and sit on the ground. I've never tried drugs – although I'd been offered some at the concert and my friend Izzie accepted them. I only drink from my bottle but feel drugged all the same. I can't stand up which is bizarrely funny.

'Whoooah.' A chant of noise comes from the left of the stage. It's loud enough that the lead singer stops singing and joins the group, cheering.

I text Mum to collect me and craw. in the opposite direction to get a fresh bottle of water and wait.

Shawna

Shitttttt, I should have paid attention when I was younger. No matter how good the sensation is, I need to pull away. I'd almost died lost in the bliss. Even in the stories, it didn't sound this good. It's better than anything. When you grow up hearing fairy tales and myths, you don't believe them. I never did. I do now!

I've broken the first two rules. Don't linger – failed. Don't be seen. I have the eyes of many humans looking at me, pointing at me. They're all wearing clothes, but I'm not. Even the man entertaining the humans is making grunting noises towards me. I turn left and right, and don't know where to go. I need to transform, but everyone is pointing. And worst of all, I've lost her — my Blood. Now her taste is on my lips, it is my job to protect her. She's the one in the short black dress, with pink legs and a straw hat. I search around. There are at least twenty girls that look like that. I try to walk through the crowd looking for her blue glow.

'Miss, come with us.' Two big men grab my arms.

'I need to find my friend,' I say.

'Everyone does. You can't walk around naked. Who shall we call?'

'Ummm.' No one. I don't know a single human. There is a number to call if we transform – I didn't memorise it, thinking it was all a joke.

I have a sheet shoved on me and am pushed into a car. Ten minutes later I arrive in a building where I'm given clothes and asked to sit in a room. 'Who shall we call for you?'

'No one,' I say again.

'Your mum?'

I shake my head.

'Your friend?'

'No, please let me go.'

They leave me in the room. I try to sneak out, but the door is locked. In the corner of the room, I take the loaned clothes off again, fold them and transform.

When the door opens, the confusion starts as I buzz out the door. I need to find my Blood and others like me. Are there other Protectors? I can't believe it's real, and not a myth. And as it's real, that means the minute my Blood dies, so do I. I have to find her. And when I do, she won't be in the same clothes.

I fly into a store and put some clothes on while the sales staff are out the back. Dressed, and human, I run out of the shop and into an alleyway.

Transforming one more time I hide the clothes in a heavy foliaged tree so I can come back and find them later.

It's so dark in the streets but I like it that way. The taste of the blood empowers me, and I feel like I can lift anything, zoom anywhere, I'm super me. But I won't be like this for long if I don't find her. I need her blood again to keep me strong. I can't remember the rules. Is anyone else's blood poison now, I've found my blood. Why haven't I paid attention? I didn't believe we could transform into humans. But we can.

I buzz around the city, looking for her and others of my kind. Disorientated, I base my search by water. The mighty Waikato River weaves its way through the centre of the town. There is a large lake which is another great feeding spot. I'd hatched in a bucket under an overgrown garden. Mosquitos only live seven days, so my siblings who hatched with me would be on their last day. Finally, I find a swarm and buzz to them. They can't remember the myths either. One tells me she thinks I'm right about poisoned blood then she makes me prove I can transform. My very own party trick. They all flap their wings as they watch me become a human, tall, with long, thin legs, and long, black hair. My face is dry and scratchy. I need to rub something on my skin. I reach out and get some mud from the river and massage that all over. When I wash it off, my skin feels better. I've never seen a human rub mud on themselves. I wonder what other protectors do. I transform back into a mosquito while my amazed admirers watch. They chat about their determination to find their chosen blood. I hope they will too because then I won't be alone. It's sad knowing all these guys will be dead in a few days.

From the first taste of her, my Blood gifts me all her knowledge and language, but also her emotions. I'm alive. I need to find my Blood to stay that way. First, I have to find some substance, and with no access to my Blood, I need fruit nectar. After a quick buzz down the river, I find a tree with some rotting fruit and fill up. I float around the city. High over the river and lake to places humans are. I see a light magical glow as I float down towards it. I find a bearded bald man coughing with a blue aura around him.

I stay with the man as he staggers north. He isn't mine, but if this man is protected, he must have his protector nearby. Once I find my Blood I can't imagine ever being out of her sight. This man is acting weird, falling all over the place. He climbs into a taxi, and I follow till we stop outside a small brick townhouse. I can't find anybody like me, so as he sleeps, I go hunting for other humans, my one with a blue glow. I go back to his place and he is gone. I can't believe I took too long. I spend the day flying around the shops and businesses looking for glows but find no one. At the end of the day I head back to his place – I'll use it as a base till I find mine or his Protector. Still, she is not there.

I'll protect him until I can protect my own. I don't think we are meant to protect others. Although while I'm watching him, my blood may die, then I will cease to exist.

As the sun goes down, the man arrives home. He's still alone but now he can walk straight. I watch him all night eating human food and staring at the box on the wall, screaming and grunting at it every now and then. As he falls asleep. I fly around the houses close by looking for blue lights, but I make sure I'm back before he wakes.

The next morning, as he catches a bus, I fly on the bus too. The man gets out at a place with lots of girls my Blood's age – which means they are my age. Some of them might have been at the concert. None of them shine.

They wear maroon and black
uniforms, so in the office, I find a
pile of them, and transform into one
before walking to the class with the
man. From the back of the class
I listen and learn. Everybody else
has something that they write on.
I explain that I'm new. The man
introduces himself as Mr Anderson
and gives me one to borrow. A
computer. Thankfully I have watched
him on his, and watched the girls and
can work out how to use it. In front of
the class of teenagers, Mr Anderson is
charismatic, he's vibrant, telling tales
with his voice going up and down,
the students hang on his words, it's
hard to believe he's the same guy,
who at home merely grunts at the TV.
I've been observing humans for days
and somehow know what they know,
things like the box on the wall is a TV,
and he is a teacher, I also can speak

French. . Wherever she is, she knows French. I can't stay in Mr Anderson's class all day, I need to find my Blood, but for now as a human I stick with a chatty girl who sits next to me, and she guides me to classes with her.

In the third class someone comes over to me, laughing and says, 'I saw you naked at the concert.'

I deny it, but they know. Seeing a tall naked teenage girl isn't something they would forget.

It was on my third night transformed, that Mr Anderson's protector finally shows up.

'Who are you?' she asks.

'I transformed and lost my Blood – but found yours. I've been looking for you.'

'I'm so embarrassed. Please don't tell anyone.' Her voice shakes.

'What happened?'

'My blood often drinks and when I taste his drink, I get amazing feelings, but Saturday night he took something else, and it sent me into a tailspin. Took me days to find my way home.'

'Welcome home.'

'So, you are lost, too? Tell me your story.'

I tell her, and thankfully she is helpful.

'Of course, you can drink any blood you want, just not my Blood. Who told you other human's blood was poisoned?' she laughs at me and gives me the address of a house in Auckland for new Protectors. 'But others blood won't keep you a Protector. You must taste your Blood to be able to transform.'

'How often?' panic flows through my body. I had wasted time hanging out with Mr Anderson and every moment without my Blood I was a moment closer to death.

We make a plan to search other schools like the one Mr Anderson teaches at, my Blood should be at one of them. Hopefully!

The next day, when Mr Anderson buses to work, we set off on our search party.

School after school we search the city.

No luck. The next day I search west and south, she heads north and east. For six hours I search but nothing. As arranged, I end up back at Mr Anderson's place and stay with him, as his Protector is lost again. She shows up late at night.

'I found her,' she says. 'Well, I found a lone Protected. She was at a school, and they all wore matching navy hats. I missed her when she got off the bus.'

I can hardly wait till the next day to find her. I have to sip nectar, while my new friend Brooke, has some of Mr Anderson's blood. He is sleeping and smiles as he revives her. Brooke protects Mr Anderson, just as he protects her.

Finally, the day that I might find my blood. According to Brooke she goes to a country school in Matamata.

'Remember, she might not be yours. She might be someone else's.'

'Are there many of us?' I ask.

'Most are based out of a house in Auckland that I visit every now and then to get the goss.'

I follow Brooke to the school, as soon as we're close I can feel her. I know she's there before I even see her blue glow. It's like a small pulse in my body, saying I'm close. Blood rushes inside me in anticipation, I can hardly focus on flying. She is sitting in class. Her school doesn't have uniforms but she's wearing blue jeans and a pink T-shirt.

'That's her.'

'I will leave you to it, maybe our paths will cross again. Thanks for looking after mine."

'Thanks for finding mine,' I say to Brooke before she flies off.

I buzz into the classroom right up close to her. She smells so good, like pear nectar. I resist having a taste. Her class is doing the same lesson I'd done earlier on in the week in maths - the silly x=apple one. It is boring and interesting at the same time. My Blood reaches down to get a pen out of her school bag and almost squashes me. I need to pay better attention. I don't mean it, but I accidentally bite her hand, just a small taste.

'Oh,' she says, pulling her hand away.

I quickly flutter up to the corner of the room. Her blood flows through my body leaving me feeling as if I'm glowing as bright as Christmas lights? I am still in my black-and-white mosquito appearance; nothing has physically changed. My Blood holds her hand, but she's smiling. Has it hurt her? I have to be careful to remember to bite at night.

At the end of school, I am determined not to lose her as Brooke had. I fly in through the bus door and wait, watching. When she gets off her bus, I follow her. She is with another girl and they're walking down the road fighting. My Blood is upset about the concert and what happened when her friends took drugs. I wonder if that was the same thing Mr Anderson and Brooke had. Whatever it is, it mustn't be good for humans or mosquitoes. In the end, my Blood runs off, leaving her friend behind. I buzz silently behind her until she turns down a driveway. The driveway has pear trees along each side. Is that why she tasted of pear nectar? She lives on a farm with cows and sheep. As she walks past each paddock she talks to the animals. Her angered footsteps becoming more like skips each animal she sees. Her animals have names. I don't understand how she can name something she is going to eat. Although she has a name and I bite her. The name I need to know is hers. I need to find out her name.

That night, she lies in bed. Her breathing changes like Mr Anderson's; she doesn't snore as he did. Her breathing is calm, blissful, inviting.

I have a snack on her, then rest. She smiles in her slumber.

From then on, we have a routine. I have found my Blood, all I have to do is keep her alive. Keep her safe and the two of us will have a long life together as long as she never finds out about me.

I think I have it made. I think it's all good, then Saturday morning arrives.

Her parents drive her into town, and she hops in a yellow and white car with the words 'driver's school' on the outside. I follow her into the car and settle in the back seat. For the next thirty minutes, we almost die in numerous ways.

Keeping this girl alive is going to be so much harder than I'd ever expected.

CASSIDY

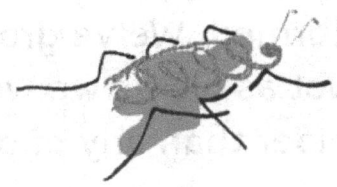

Cassidy

Dust settles, no tumble weeds roll down the old frontier town. The sun has risen in the sky, mid-day looming.

The saloon is empty – even the jail is vacant. The whole town stands around, watching the two cowboys who are back-to-back, guns in hand.

My sister and I are closer than most sisters. That's because we've gone through a transformation together, extending our lives at the same waterhole with two very different cowboys. Hours later, we had both transformed. We've grown old together. Not as old as we would've liked, but older than any of our other siblings.

Sadie Dallas has done this to us. This death sentence – my sister or I. Beau or Colt.

Our Bloods, guns in hands, step - three, two, one.

Transformed as humans, we sisters hold each other as the bullets fly.

'Let me stop them,' she whispers. We had tried all night to come up with a way to stop this duel. Alas, no luck.

The projectiles pass each other in the middle. I tightened my grip on Bella. Which one of our Blood's will marry Sadie, the twice widowed cowgirl?

Whose blood will spill, leaving us untransformable. Colt's blood has not even spilt when I feel my power drain, my body shrink, one hit and he is gone – I am gone. A bullet through his heart.

Bella cries as I fly to her shoulder, but her Blood is hit too, she transforms.

We fly above the scene, wagons pulled to clear away our lifelines. We have seven days to watch over their deaths and families' tears. Sadie, who they have died for, moves on with the county cobbler.

A waste of four lives.

JANICE

Janice

On my seventh day I've given up finding my Blood. But then I come across a boy who's being bullied. There are three guys looming over the poor child. One steals his glasses, another one tears his top. It is shit and the third one just stands there, saying nasty, nasty words. Not being able to handle it, I buzz around, wanting to help. I start biting the bullies; they scratch as my saliva spreads around the body. I finally buzz to the last tormentor, and neither of us are expecting it. As his blood pulses through my body, it sends shocks like a live wire, waking me up. He lets go of the boy he is intimidating and dances as if he's drunk. He lies on the ground, looks up at the clouds, finding shapes in them. The boy who is being bullied snatches his glasses and runs away as the tyrants try to work out why their friend is acting insane. The other two help their fallen leader home, and I follow, hoping the bullied boy avoids them next time.

Like it or not, I am bound to that loser now, wish it'd been the boy being bullied – I would have to deal to my Blood's mates. Every seven days, I would have to reach out to this idiot to keep me alive.

That was when he was sixteen, now he's twenty-nine, he has one marriage under his belt and is living with a much younger lady. She's lovely - how has a nice girl fallen for a man who's so evil? His last relationship was so toxic I was constantly calling the police on him. It is our Blood whom we protect for life - not their naïve love interests. It's getting harder and harder to replenish on his blood because I don't enjoy being drunk - normal Blood Protectors take the blood feed while their Blood sleeps, but I can't do that. I wait till just as he's about to open his first drink of the day. 11 am if I'm lucky.

It's currently 11 pm and his girlfriend is crying in the door of their rental house. He made her drive him to the pub so she could drive him home, screwed her and then he got up and said, 'I'm going out.'

'You're drunk, you can't drive.' she says snatching his keys off him.

'You're not the boss of me,' he says, grabbing the keys back. He pushes her out of the way and a little harder than he plans to. 'Where are you going?' She asks from the floor.

'Out,' he says, he grabs the keys and drives off, leaving her in the door crying. He's drunk, not only a risk to himself, but a risk to anybody else who goes near his vehicle. He speeds along the 50 km zone at 90 km an hour; I don't know how he thinks he's driving. He's winding from his side of the road to the other. A man on a bicycle gets out of his way just in time. I know I have to do something. He's gonna kill someone. I bite him. He acts even more drunk than he normally does. I wait till he stops at

the lights then I bite his face, into
his cheeks, his neck and hand. He
swats away at me. I keep at him,
avoiding his hits like a mole in the
'wack a mole' game. Eventually, he's
going to kill me in the meantime. The
police come up the other way. He
doesn't see them. He is still too busy
trying to hit me. As the sirens turn
on, he swears and instinctively puts
his foot down on the accelerator. His
face is all puffy. With alcohol ruling
his actions he doesn't know what
he's doing. I quickly fly out his open
window as his car plunges towards
the riverbank. He goes straight off
the edge. It's not even five minutes
when I begin to feel his energy
within myself disappear. His blood
still pumps inside me, but my aura
has gone. I can no longer transform.
All I can do now is educate. I fly
around local clusters of mosquitoes,

telling them my story, hoping they will pass it on to future generations, and then they will know what to do with a situation like I've been in.

BETTY

Betty

There are guidelines, rules, and life or death decisions. Love, emotions, and feelings can't be constrained by restrictions. I never expected to fall in love, aside from the love that I had for the one I protected. You see, my lifeline is connected to her. When Bethany Jane Johnstone dies, I too will die. My entire existence depended on her breathing and the flowing blood inside her body. Blood, which is liquid gold to me.

The number one rule, Bethany can never know that I exist. That I protect and safeguard her. I have given her everything since I found her as a three-year-old. I became a three-year-old girl too, and we have aged together ever since.

That was also the day I met Bethany's twin brother, Karl James Johnstone. I've also known him since he was three. I was there when he fell off his bike learning to ride. Bethany didn't fall off her bike because I was there to protect her. As the twins turned 14, Bethany became interested in boys. Karl was not interested in girls, however, when he became interested, they weren't interested in him. Their loss.

For their sixteenth birthday, the twins had a dress up party. I had watched these guys grow up. Kept Bethany safe for thirteen years. I had one night out from the shadows. I would still be near; I would still keep Bethany safe. I had watched them have fun at school dances, but watched nobody dance with Karl. I wanted to go so Karl could have somebody to dance with on his birthday. But most of all, I wanted to play human for one night. But if I had known what would happen, I would never have played human at all.

Dressed as a bunny, I wear hot pink tights, pink tutu, black crop top and a bunny mask covering my face. I let my long black hair down and loosely plait my pigtails flowing down my back. I walk through the front door and Mr Johnstone sings out, 'Well, hello Betty Bunny!'

I didn't have a human name. Why not Betty? 'Hi,' I hop into

the party. Bethany has a group of friends all around her. There're some masked boys dotted around the beige-on-beige lounge suite. I don't recognise any of them as Karl, or Bethany's friends. I slide over to the closest one and say, 'Do you mind if I sit here?" He pats the couch beside him and I sit down. He is throwing dice up and catching it. 'Do you mind if I play?'

'I'm not playing a game,' he held onto his die tight.

'Let's make it a game,' I grin. 'First person to roll to 20.'

'You're on,' he rolls the dice.

Our giggles echo around the room. Other groups laugh over the music beating away. People started dancing, the dice throwing boy dressed up as Buzz Lightyear asks me if I want to dance. Of course, I want to dance. I could hear people

talking about my height. I don't care;
I'm dancing.

To start with, we are nowhere near
each other, but we dance for an hour,
two hours, by the third hour he is
holding me; it's wonderful. We laugh
as we do silly dance movements;
like the twist and chicken dance,
we completely ignore everybody else
in the room. I'm not even watching
Bethany. Mr Johnstone turns the
music off and says time to go
everybody. Everybody starts leaving.
It is then that I see Bethany crying.
I take a step towards her, but she
doesn't know who I am. I need to
change. What to do? I have paid
no attention to her. I fly out to the
playground, which was three houses
along. I walk behind a tree and
transform. Then I pass back through
the bathroom window that is always
left open.

The boy Bethany had liked, had kissed somebody else on her sweet 16th birthday. She thought she would get him. Love was so horrible. It completely ruined her party.

She should have celebrated surviving her challenging sixteen years. She hadn't fallen off the bridge on holiday in Australia when she was twelve. She hadn't died when her kayak tipped over on a river and a stranger (that's me) pulled her to shore and did CPR. All those times that she hadn't died needed celebrating. I'm focused again and keep her safe, but I can't protect her from boys.

She is wrapped in her dad's lap, crying. Mum comes in, swaps with her dad and stays with her the night. The next day she stays in bed, but on the Monday, her parents make her go back to school. I follow her. There is no mention of the party or boys or anything.

At the end-of-year, the twins head to a party at the beach. I know I need to have my wits about me. I need to be focused. Bethany is swimming with some friends, a group of boys stay behind on the shore. I can't follow the girls out, but I watch them hovering behind the boys. Joshua Smith turns to Karl and ask after his sister. Karl doesn't know, but I suspect she likes Joshua. The boys start talking about girls and then my world is shaken. Karl says, 'There's only one girl for me, but I don't know how to find her. I met her at my party and she had a mask on the whole time.'

'Sounds straight out of a fairy-tale.'

'Seriously, did you see her? The bunny? I've got photos of me holding her on the dance floor. We even played this really neat dice game. I just don't know who she is.'

She is me. My dream night out with somebody was with Karl. Buzz Lightyear's voice sounded higher pitched; did I have that effect on him? Was that how I'd not known?

When the girls arrive back, Joshua takes Bethany for a walk. I follow, and by the time they return to the group, they are holding hands. Melissa skips up to Karl and asks him to go for a walk. Bethany nods to him. He gets up and walks off. I want to follow him. I get this feeling in my stomach. Suddenly I hate Melissa. Weird as I don't even know her. She's been around but not close, but she has just become enemy number one. I want her away from Karl. When they come back, they are not holding hands, which makes me feel happier than it should have. That night when Bethany finally puts her phone down and sleeps, I fly off to Karl's room. I've never been in there, just hovered at the door. I fly to where Karl's head is and look back towards the entrance. I can see his photos. He has photos of him and Bethany snorkelling in Fiji. That had been a fun trip. Photos of the four of them snowboarding the Remarkables. It was horrible - so cold I could hardly keep up with them. I transformed at night-time, wearing many clothes sitting in front of the Hyatt fire all night, just to warm up. But there were photos of me and him on his 16th birthday. We were sitting on the couch together, dancing, holding hands, his arms around my waist. I spend far too long reminiscing as I stare at them. After an hour still in his room I realise I have a serious problem, so I fly back to the room I belong in. Out of sight but not out of mind, I think of Karl all night. The next day, the twins join a group of friends at the mall. I can't help it, I put on my pink tights and skirt and black T-shirt, no mask. I'm Betty bunny without the bunny and I walk past Karl.

'Betty.'

'Hi, do I know you?' I ask as if I don't.

'Dress up party, I was Buzz Lightyear.'

'Oh my gosh,' I fake surprise.

'I never got your number.'

'That was because I don't have a phone.'

'No phone? Really! Would you like to come to the movies with us?'

I nod.

He holds my hand, and I follow as we walk around the counter and into the old but magnificent embassy theatre.

Karl buys two tickets, one for each
of us, and a couple's popcorn pack.
I don't eat things like popcorn, but
I can always drop it under the
seat. Many times, at the movies I've
hidden under the seats, they are
disgusting.

Melissa gives us the evil looks, but
Bethany – who is never allowed to
see me in human form, smiles at
us. Before we enter the cinema, she
walks over. 'Who's this?" she asked,
looking at our connected hands.

'This is my Betty,'

'I'm his Betty.' I smile, looking at
him, not her.

'You look familiar,' she says.
Could she remember one of the
times I'd saved her? We were only
young then. I've aged as she has.
'Seriously, there is something about
you. Where do you go to school?'

'I am home schooled,' I tell her a lie. I go to all her classes with her, study German and art – as she does.

'Bethany,' Karl growls with his voice and eyes.

She takes her brother's hint and leaves us to it. We walk in and sit in the back row with the rest of their school friends. Bethany is kissing her boyfriend. I want to kiss her brother. By being here I'm playing with fire – hopefully, Bethany wouldn't get burnt.

The biggest issue is by the end of the night I've ignited the fire, fallen deeper in love than the characters on the rom-com we are meant to have watched. But Karl and I are only watching each other. Every so often, he lets go of my hand to move hair off my face, or I playfully tap his nose, like his mother does to her husband.

He smiles at me and when the on-screen couple have their first kiss, so do we. The night is magical, but as soon as the credits roll, I know I have to transform or lie. I stand when he does and wrap my arms around him, kissing him until he pulls away from me. I leave the row first, run out the door, into the women's toilets and transform, leaving my clothes in the bin.

The car trip home is horrible. Bethany questioned Karl all about me and Karl did not know any of the answers. By the end of the night's journey, he is in tears. 'I don't know how to find her.'

I am standing on his back. Close to him and he is crying for me.

That night, well, I float between the rooms of the two people that I love. Trying to come up with a plan. No matter how I look at it, there only seemed to be one solution because I can't give him up. I need him, love him. I need a plan to love him. Protectors are allowed to be with humans. In fact, there is a bar in Auckland where they get drunk and up to all sorts of horrible things and I mean, they get drunk on blood.

I could go to the lake house and ask for help. So long as they don't ask the right questions, they will help me with money, guardianship, anything I need. I just need them to think that my Blood needs help, not that I'm in love with a human. They need to not know that I'm breaking the rules.

The next night, while everyone sleeps, I fly to the petrol station and hitch a ride in the car to Auckland. The big grey house is full of protectors, sharing stories and drinking their Bloody Barry cocktails. I have my sob story all set up; I need to attend my Blood's school because her life is at risk.

A week later, my new pretend mum Gabby comes over and takes me to the local school. Gabby has all the paperwork and documents for me. The exact same school and classes as Bethany- only Gabby didn't know that. Gabby organises a two-bedroom flat and sets me up with clothes, furniture, perfume, a cell phone, even with a laptop. One problem we Protectors have is our ridiculously long, thin legs, which means finding clothes that fit in the lost property box is very unlikely. Gabby has brought me a stockpile of jeans in three different colours, and three different shades of blue. Long tights and long dresses, she also gives me some fancy shoes with no heels, so if I wear them, it looks like high heels without the height. Of course, Karl is five foot five, and he hasn't complained about my height yet. And he spent a lot of time talking about me. I didn't mean to overhear, but my Blood left her door open and his room is next to hers.

Gabby heads back to Auckland, so I drop my façade, and I settled into my flat, which is the next street over from the Johnstone's house. The first thing I have to do is run into Karl again and get his phone number, now that I have a phone. I get dressed in a faded pair of blue jeans and a surf T-shirt, put on some sandals. Karl is going to go to the dairy for milk. He runs into me three minutes later.

'Hey Karl,' I say, reaching out to him. He tippy toes up to kiss me. The minute our lips part, he pulls out his phone and says, 'Please give me your number. I hate having a girlfriend I can't arrange catch ups with.'

'I'm **your** girlfriend?' I ask raising my eyes.

'You are my girlfriend, right?'

'Yes.' I feel like I'm going to fly, and that is in human form.

He holds my hand while he purchases the milk, and together we walk back to his house, hand-in-hand. We talk about the movie and he tells me about his sister, how he loves to hate her and hates to love her. He really loves to love her. I already know that. He opens the front door for me. For the first time in thirteen years, I walk in as an invited guest to the house that has always been my home. The Johnstones make me feel very welcome. They try to give me cookies. Of course, I don't eat human food, but there is an apricot in the fruit bowl and I ask if I can have that instead. Karl throws it at me and I catch it, can I catch his heart.

Bethany walks out. 'I swear I know you. There's something about you.'

'You should know her. She's my girlfriend.'

'Well, that's great news. Hurt him and I'll hurt you,' she threatens.

'Should I have said the same thing to Joshua?' Karl asks.

'Who's Joshua?' the parents ask.

'Sorry,' Karl says, hiding behind my shoulder.

'We're going to the beach today. Would you like to join us?' Mrs Johnstone asks me.

'Yes please, I'll call mum and see if it's okay.' I pretend to call and then tell them I can go. Joshua has been invited too, and they are getting ready. I dash home to get ready. Gabby left me a beach bag with togs, towels, sunscreen and, of all things, insect repellent – as if that works. I spray it and it is just water, thankfully.

The Johnstones pick me up from my house thirty minutes later. They are sorry to have only just missed mum,(sure) and Karl and I sit in the back of the car and hold hands. Today will give us more to talk about. But I still have to stay near Bethany. She is my job, Karl my hobby.

All six of us have a swim together, the three couples holding hands. Mrs Johnstone snaps away taking photos. Karl will now have more pics of us for his room. Joshua is tall, well, 6.1 not 6.4 like me. It's embarrassing being that tall, but if they ever met Gabby, they would understand. I wasn't sure if our long legs are so we could tower over a crowd to keep our bloods safe, or because in our original form we have long, long legs.

The next three weeks are amazing. By the time we start year thirteen, I feel like a member of the Johnstone family. Karl is my forever. I have to be careful when they tell me stories about their holidays and life experiences, seeing I already know the stories, and when they ask about my experiences, I make sure they aren't the ones they know. Twice I say I've been to things that Bethany was at, and maybe that's where she'd seen me. We'd been to the same shows, movies, concerts, but I figured that was acceptable. As school starts, Bethany spends more time with me, not her old friends who are getting heavier into drugs. So you see, my presence in her life is helping keep her safe. She'd always been my best friend: she just hadn't known it. She comes to me about all her problems, and I make some problems up to go to her about, and the three of us study together.

Everything is a dream, and the year flys by. Karl is nagging to meet my mum. So I have to call Gabby to come down and play fake mum for a while. She comes on days that I know Bethany plays sports. I have a fake birthday where mum, the Johnstones and Karl head out. I have to keep Bethany away because, as my Blood, Gabby will see the protected glow around Bethany. The biggest problem I have is that mosquitoes weren't meant to have emotions, and Gabby knows I'm in love.

'Listen, Betty,' Gabby says when we're alone after a visit. 'Others have fallen in love and left their Blood. It has never worked out and we will not support you.'

'I understand. He's just a boyfriend,' I lie.

'No, he's not. Watch yourself.'

One thing going my way is Joshua. He adores Bethany and will keep her safe if I'm distracted with Karl. When they walk down the street, Joshua walks along the roadside protecting her. I do, however, miss the fact that Bethany is no longer interested in Joshua. She is spending a lot of time on her phone. I assumed it was Joshua, but when he asks me Monday what she'd been doing all weekend and why he hadn't been able to get hold of her, I realise I had some investigating to do.

I watch her phone from the corner of her bed that night as she texts a stranger I haven't vetted. A new boy at a different school, a boys only Catholic school. How bad can a catholic boy be?

Tuesday after school, she ditches us to meet the new boy. I ditch Karl, to follow her. I feel sick as I watch him make moves on her. Joshua has never made moves Karl hasn't made. This guy is vulgar. Catholic has her half naked in his tree house as the sun sets.

The next day at school, she is back with Joshua. I have a class that day, where I'm not with either of the twins, so I skip it and fly to the catholic school to watch that boy.

His name's Ralph, like the Muppet, and he is a real life Muppet. He is telling his friends how he slept with three girls over the weekend, and somehow has pictures of them all, including Bethany. She is topless, and it looks as though they'd done more than they had.

I stay away from school for the rest of the day, and tail Ralph, learning all I can about him, including his phone pin number. The minute he leaves his phone alone, I transform and unlock his phone. I send messages to all the girls, and his sister showing them what he's been doing, before I delete all of his photos. Scorned women will do more to him than I ever could.

By the time I fly back home, Bethany is in tears. I know she won't talk to me as a human, so I buzz in the corner. Karl is concerned because he doesn't know where I am. He isn't losing me, he never will.

I spent the next few days doing what I can for Bethany - flowers in her room, opening the correct pages in her texts books to help her study go smoother.

Bethany ended things with Joshua, even though he is perfect. She doesn't think she is good enough for him. I'm spending an equal amount of time with the twins, the three of us go everywhere together. I love these two. And Karl loves me as much as I love him. Not only does he tell me all the time, but he also tells anyone he meets about our real love.

It is mid-year of year 13 when my world collapses. It's too much, and the reason I start writing this story. I should never have transformed for the party, because now I have to make a choice, love or death.

Careers Day, and I've always known Bethany wants to be a marine scientist and study in Dunedin. Karl wants to be a doctor, and I thought he would study in Dunedin too. But he says he can't leave his parents, and he wants to study in Auckland. I planned to study Marine Biology with Bethany. I've dreamt of the three of us in Dunedin together. I have to keep Bethany safe, and love Karl and I can't do both from two different islands. I can't flicker between the two of them like I do now when they are in different classes, or rooms in the house. I have to choose life with Bethany or love with Karl.

What would you choose? Well I don't have the luxury of choice. If I don't taste Bethany's blood every seven days I loose the ability to transform – and die of old age in seven days.

DANA

Daria

'**A** mosquito!' Mum screams like it's a man wired up with a bomb vest and his finger is on the explosion button.

'I'm okay, mum.' I watch her as she runs around asking strangers at the carols by candlelight night if they have any insect repellent. I can't help but laugh at how she looks like a cartoon character. And they say I have ADHD – the apple hasn't fallen far here.

A mosquito lands on me. I'm about to swat it away when I laugh as my veins feel all tingly. The mosquito flies away, but before it disappears into the darkness, I swear it looks at me as if to say, 'Thanks and by the way, your mum is crazy.'

'You're welcome,' I say to the mosquito.

The boy in front of me turns to see who I'm talking to. I laugh louder and his cheeks flush. Like smiles, laughter is contagious. His name's Raymond. I've known him the three years we've been at high school, but this is the closest we've been to communicating. Mum will ruin that in three, two, one!

I cough at all the insect repellent being sprayed on me. The boy looks again and rolls his eyes, the twinkle from before truly lost now.

'You saved my life mum – sit down. It's your favourite carol.' She sits and together, and louder than others around us we sing 'Pa rum pum pum pum'

I hold my finger over the small hole where the mosquito has been. Mum gets invested in singing as I do, and I successfully hide the bite mark from her. Mum and I sing with our candles up in the air, waving side to side. I catch Raymond turning to look at me again. He smiles. I should talk to him one day as he is not as annoying as the other boys in the class.

Dana

It happened – it really happened to meeeeee. Can't believe I found my

Blood – her blood was amazing - pulsing in my body, waking all my human senses. I watch her from a tree up high – see the other mosquitoes swarming around the singing humans, hoping to find their Blood. I've found my one and I won't let her out of my sight.

Daria

I hate having haemophilia. People look at me like I have a disease - they don't invite me to play sports because if I get hurt, they become guilty. As if having haemophilia isn't bad enough, it tends to mainly affect boys – so why am I one of the few females with it! So over it! A few times I have tried to hide it – played football or such and ended up in hospital with a week off school.

So today I sit on the seat safely watching the other students having fun at lunch time. My book is on my lap, but I have been on the same page for twenty minutes and have no idea what's happened to Kenzie, the main character.

I let no one see my eyes floating away from the letters to the footie game, which has stopped. Raymond is being supported, blood dripping down his leg towards another bench seat. He says something to the guys half carrying him, and they look at me before changing routes.

'Do you mind?' Raymond asks, slumping down beside me. Even if I did, I would be a cow to tell him to drag his bloody ass elsewhere.

'You okay?' I ask.

'Sure, a little blood never hurt anyone....' he gulped, 'sorry.'

'Don't worry.' I let him off the hook. 'Back in a second.'

In the bathroom I grab paper towels, wet them, then race back to him to apply on his gash.

'Awww.' He breathes through gritted teeth.

'Trust me – I know how to stop blood.'

'Thanks,' he smiles, relaxing his body a little. 'So, you like Snoopy's Christmas?'

'Who doesn't? It's catchy, even historic for people who like that sort of stuff, and well it's all about the joy of Christmas.'

'True,' he laughs.

We chat until the lunch bell rings.

In class, my best friend Izzie asks me why I'd been with Raymond during her netball practice. I explain about his leg.

'If that's all it is, why does he keep looking at you? Maybe he likes you.'

'He thinks I am weird. He saw mum being overprotective last week.'

'Oh! She really is over the top.'

Dana

I watch my Blood slowly falling for Raymond. I wish I could have a boyfriend. That isn't in my job description – protect your Blood – your lifeline. Taste her once a week and live as long as she does. What if my drinking her blood causes her to die? I'd looked up her condition- one that meant her precious blood doesn't clot up, she dies, I die. I need her to live not just so that I can, but already I care for her. I need some advice. I need to find the legend of the lake house. As soon as she falls asleep, I fly to the North Shore looking for the other protectors. To our eyes others like me have a red glow, so I just look for the glow until I see it.

'Hey – I am newly transformed – can you help me find the others?'

'Sure, follow me,' she says. I follow her across the street to a house where we stop outside.

'Aren't you coming?' I ask.

'No, I'm not welcome there.' She says before buzzing away.

Why would someone not be welcome? Will I?

I transform and knock on the door.

'We got a wriggler,' a blonde calls, passing me a dress. I slide it on and follow her inside.

The house is elegant and four others like me stand around a table drinking what looks like blood from a tall glass with celery sticking out of it. We all have long legs, long hair and long noses.

'Come, tell us all about you.'

They huddle in closer.

Daria

After school Thursdays all my friends have netball so I head home alone. 'Duck!' A high-pitched scream awakens my curiosity. A football hits the back of my head. I rub it and bend down to throw it back to the kids who'd tried to warn me.

Ouch, that hurt, I turn back to the road to head away from school when this time I hear my name, 'Daria'

Raymond is rushing towards me over the zebra crossing. 'Hi,'

My stomach does a little flip before my brain takes over. He normally catches the bus out of town - why is he here?

'Hi,' I stumble.

Panting and puffing he catches up to me, but he doesn't say anything for a while until his breathing slows. He takes a sip of water then stands up straight and again says 'Hi.'

He's the one who called me, but he's too busy recovering from his run to talk. Awkwardly I don't know what to say so I stand still till finally I ask the question that's most running through my mind. How come you're not on your bus?

He holds up a finger as he takes another sip of his water. More uncomfortable silence is absorbed in the meter distance between us. Some other kids walk past, one of them says 'Raymond and Daria, sitting up a tree.'

I hope my cheeks aren't as red as Raymond's. He has one more sip of his water and then says 'I'm staying at my gran's tonight. I wonder if I could walk you home.

I didn't know if you knew where I lived. I may not live anywhere near his gran's, the fact that he wants to walk me home was too exciting to get bogged down on the details. 'That would be great.' I say, 'Shall we have a rest first?'

'I'm good,' he puffs.

Right turn into Carlton Ave and walk. 'What did you think of that last class?' he asks.

We had English together and we watched the movie Boy. 'Taika's a bit of an egg.' I laugh.

'He's a brilliant egg,' he says. At least we both paid attention to the movie and enjoyed the egg scene in there. It also broke that awkwardness we had, talking about movies that we liked, actors that we liked. Our chat changes to music as we turn onto Guyton Street. Raymond walks even closer to me. I go to step over a driveway, and Raymond puts his hand out to stop me as a car exits. I hadn't even seen it. I'm normally more alert about my surroundings. After that, one of his arms stays around my waist. Is it because he is being overprotective? My whole life everybody's been overprotective of me. Or is it because he likes me? We are close to my home now, I don't know if I should let him know where I live, I know I'll be awake all night wondering why he chose to walk this way so I ask, no harm right? 'Why did you want to walk with me today?"

'I just wanted to spend more time with you. I really enjoy it when we chat.'

'I'm almost at home.' I chuckle, wishing I wasn't.

'Bugger,' he says.

'Why bugger?' I ask. He turns red, the same colour as the letterbox we are standing beside.

'Is there a park or somewhere near here? We can chat a bit longer?' he looks around. As it happens, we are near an alleyway with a park down further. I tell him, 'but I just have to message my mum.'

The edges of his mouth curl up. I bet he is remembering how incredibly overprotective my mother is of me. I text her as we walk through the alleyway past the lovely smelling jasmine. We arrive at the park, and I sit on the swing, I think that he will sit beside me, but he doesn't. He comes behind me and gently pushes my back. Mum never lets me go on the swings, if I fall off, hurt myself, who knows how long the recovery will be. I pray Raymond isn't thinking like that. I feel like such a daredevil, swinging higher and higher and laughing. My laughing is at a new level. When I'm high enough, he stops pushing me and sits on the next swing. He quickly gets to the same height as me, and in the same rhythm, we swing smiling at each other. Slowly, I stop swinging my legs, he copies me until we are just slightly swaying. I jump off and stand in front of him. He twiddles his legs around me a little. It is wrong to go if he wants to spend more time with me. I show him that I like him to. He steps off his swing and puts his hands on my hips. I put my arms on his too and then lay my head on his chest. No-one has ever held me before. I don't know which of us has the larger grin. We stay like that, hearts beating and thrilling off each other's energy

until I hear the worst possible noise
in the world.

'Daria!' Mum screams.

Raymond takes the largest step
ever away from me.

'Mum this is my friend Raymond.'

'Enough of that!' she snaps. 'You
look like you're more than friends.'
She drags me away.

I reach out my hand to Raymond
and wave.

He waves back. I bet I've lost
him now. How can I possibly come
back from that. Each step away
from Raymond I feel more and more
fatigued, by the time I get home
I curl into bed missing dinner. I'd
rather starve than have a lecture
anyway.

Dana

Raymond smiles after Daria disappears, so sweet. Watching them is like watching a TV romance. I can't wait to see the next chapter at school tomorrow. Daria is safe with her mum, so I follow Raymond for a while. He's so taken with her. He floats into the dairy and I watch as he buys chocolate 'These are for my girlfriend,' he tells the lady serving him. He's not gonna let an overprotective mum get in the way of the budding young romance.

I fly off leaving Raymond in *Daria dreamland* and head back to work. One of the other protectors' Blood is a doctor. The doctor's house is huge with a crammed library of medical books. When Daria sleeps that night, I go to my brethren's Blood Protected house. She lets me in, and I read until daylight streams through the sheer white curtains. I now know how to stop external bleeding. I need to learn more about replacement factor 8, and internal bleeding, I'm still not sure on. I fly home. Daria's mum has gone to work early. Daria's alarm is playing in her room. She hasn't turned it off which is weird. I fly in and the first thing I smell is blood, lots of blood, her brown skin is pale. I transform in a pile of her clothes and dress. I don't care what she'll think if she wakes up to a stranger in her clothes. I shake her to wake her up, 'Wake up Daria, wake up.' She doesn't. I reach for her phone to unlock it with her private six-digit number that I've memorised and dial 111. I unlock the front door and open it wide before I transform back to a mosquito so I can follow her.

It takes ten minutes for the ambulance to arrive and I follow them to the hospital. And I can't go inside the hospital - too much bug spray. It will kill me being away from Daria. I find a shaded area outside the main doors to the hospital and wait and watch. Daria's mum dashes in and I wait. Hours later Daria's mum comes back out in tears. She's dramatic, surely nothing's happened but I feel different. Stress? I try to transform to a human, but I can't.

GABBY

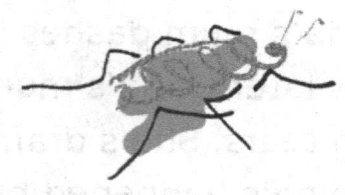

Winner of sci-fi/fantasy short story
at the International Writers Workshop
2023

Gabby

He always looks so peaceful when
he sleeps. I'd be too anxious. Anxious
about something happening to him
while I wasn't alert. He does a
loud snore and wakes up. It's so
funny when he wakes himself up.

Thankfully, he doesn't see me -
A naked woman standing in his
wardrobe amongst his crisp white
shirts and black suits.

My Blood's such a geek who
complains he'll never get a girlfriend.
He doesn't know that I'm always right
here for him. My legs are almost
longer than his whole body. Out of his
league, he'd say. I have long white
hair; he has spiky auburn hair framing
his chubby face. I'd hate it if he got a
girlfriend, I'd be jealous, but he only
interacts on the computer.

Once he's pulled his white sheets
up to his chin, his soft snoring starts
again, I transform. Flying over I land
on his shoulder, walk my way down
his arm to his exposed forearm. The
right side tonight. I stick my proboscis
into his skin, and I hear his joyful
sigh as his blood electrifies me, giving
me strength, keeping me alive, past

what would normally have been a seven-day life. So far, he's extended my life for thirty years.

Gavin

I have the longest shower before getting dressed, and re dressed. My first date and I'm a forty-seven-year-old – pathetic. I settle for jeans and a black polo shirt. Black sneakers and socks. I lock my ground-floor apartment and I walk to the central city with enough time to get some cologne. Trialling smells, I spray them on a store card, floral, musk – eww that one smells like fly spray! I'm running out of time. Spray one last one - perfect, fresh but still masculine. I want to be early.

The older I get the more I rely on glasses, but I don't want to be that cliche IT geek. If I get a seat close to the door, I'll be able to see her easily. She said she'd wear a daffodil. But as I arrive at the cafe, I spot her sitting in the corner, her yellow brooch is big enough that I can see it without needing glasses, so I rip them off and shove them in my pocket.

She stands up and is taller than me. Her daffodil brooch, taking up half of the left side of her top. She's definitely out of my league, so beautiful. I don't have the looks or charm to reel her in. She smiles all the same. I sit beside her, awkward silence as we read the menu I had memorised last night.

Food ordered; she starts talking of travel. I've never left the country, but I've watched lots of shows, so I think of things to ask her and not come across weird about certain spots in each destination she's visited. I don't know what else to say.

Towards the end she says 'You are so witty, Gavin. Can we meet again?'

Me – witty? 'That'd be great.' We plan to meet in the same place next week.

In the cafe doorway she leans in for a hug. Surprisingly her lips land on mine. It's over before I can react. The night's a win.

Floating, I stop to cross the road, put my hand in my pocket and pull out my glasses. They're shattered beyond repair; I must have sat on them in the cafe.

A huge force hits me.

Gabby

I hadn't meant to push him with such strength. I'd been angry about his date. I wasn't even his species. Well, I look like human, but I need blood to survive – his Blood. He was going to get run over – I had to save him. I am after all, his blood protector.

I can feel his breathing, his blood pulsing around his body. I know that he's fine, but he's hit his head. A lady rushes over to us. She's on the phone calling for help.

'Can you hear me? You've been hurt but I'm getting you help.' She keeps talking to him until the ambulance arrives and stays with him as the doors shut. I need to be with my Blood but I have to stay behind, explaining what happened to the police.

Afterwards, I go into a dark alleyway, transform back to a mosquito, and fly home. He isn't there. I know he'll be at a hospital, but I don't know which one, so I have to wait.

I wait and wait.

While I wait, I don't waste time. I jump on his computer and investigate everything I can on the woman who kissed him. I search, hidden deep in pages I find it, name changed but I was right. She's a scammer. Prays on single men, taking whatever money she can from them.

I print all the articles I find on her and mail them to my Blood. Then continue the wait for him to come home.

I wait. And wait. If he's not home in seven days, I die.

On the sixth day he comes home via a taxi. He sits opening his mail, both digital and paper. He scans the mail from me and throws it straight in the rubbish. Does he not believe me?

His phone rings, 'Hi, yeah, I'm
home fine.' A little silence and
he adds, 'That would be amazing.
Okay, see you soon.'

He hangs the phone up and stands,
walks over to his bed, fluffs his
pillows. He steps to the lounge, fluffs
more pillows, puts away dishes from
the dishwasher, then starts a load
of washing and walks outside. A pair
of scissors in his hands, he snips
flowers from his small garden. Back
inside he puts them in a vase on the
table.

I realise she's coming over. He's
already fallen in love with her and
doesn't care what I printed out. How
can I save him from her now?

The doorbell chimes. I should've
been out there. Could've scared her
off. He opens the door and the smell
of perfume wafts in, mixing with his
cologne.

'Hi," he smiles, looking her in the eyes and away from her curvy body.

'Hello,' she giggles back at him. They sound like lovesick teenagers. Relief flows in me as I see it's not the scamming cafe woman. It's the ambulance lady. I know nothing about her. What if she's worse for him.

They sit on the couch and turn the TV on. She slides into his arms, like he's been holding her forever and they watch episode six together. She must've been visiting him when he was in hospital. After the episode they have tea together. She's made him home-made chicken soup. They watch another two episodes of the show before she finally leaves. But she doesn't leave alone. I fly into the back of her car. The minute she's out of the driveway she's on the phone.

'He's perfect! I just love him,' she says.

'I hope you didn't tell him you love him!'

'Don't be silly. I don't want to scare him. He's the first man I've met for ages that appears genuine.' She then talks all about his body language and analyses every minute that they've been together. She drives to a two-bedroom house. It's clean and tidy like his house, photos on the wall. She's widely travelled and doesn't appear to have children. Once she's asleep I look through her bank records. Nothing dodgy, she seems legit. The more I look, the more I like her.

Next day I follow her to work. She stops to help a crying child, gently puts a plaster on the girl's cut and then gives her a sweet. She leaves money for a homeless man, says sorry when someone else bumps into her, and then gives blood. I transform into a human and bump into her.

'Hey you stopped that hit and run.' She remembers me and she gives me a hug. 'Thank you for saving my man, and for introducing us.'

'Any time,' I say walking away.

Is it my fault they are together, I couldn't let him die. If he dies, I too die. I fly back home where from my hidden corner I watch their love bloom. I had thought I'd be jealous, but turns out not only do I like her, I love how happy she makes him.

All my investigating into the woman who crossed his path, everything I did to keep him safe, I didn't realise.

It wasn't until a year later, blood all over the bathroom floor, that I realised she wasn't the threat.

Acknowledgements

My team, Anna McKersey, Melissa Gunn, Val Carpenter, Melodie Lindsay.

My critique crew, Jess, Jade, Kara Claire, Nic, Sarah, Ashley, Mayur, Kynan, Shan, Darien and Tremaine.

My rocks, Tonchi, Marco, Lucas, Frankie, Mum, Diana and Glen and my Pram Fam XXX

My sanity, Tania, Janelle, Julie, Kim, Cinnamon, Anna, Casie, Ange, Melissa, Beca and Liz

A Dyslexic friendly, easy to read collection of short stories set in the world of the Blood Protectors.

Thanks to the team at Te Pae Tawhiti Awards for selecting this book as a finalist in 2025 for Outstanding Achievement for a Collection/Anthology and to the International Writers Workshop for selecting the story Gabby as winner of sci-fi/fantasy short story in 2023.

About the author
Sue Carpenter

Sue is a Junior Fiction and Young Adult Author.

She doesn't want her readers to need a dictionary to fall into her imaginary worlds. Sue is not ready to grow up yet and keeps her mind young by writing for children and spending time with her three sons. To find more of Sue's work follow her on Instagram susieleenz

The Black Manor

Belinda's uncle has taught her everything she knows about animals but when he suddenly dies, has he taught her enough to be able to run his pet business? Belinda suspects her uncle's staff are up to more than just breeding parrots so now she has to learn to care for new animals. Caged kiwis and strange sounding boxes have Belinda on edge. What secrets are the staff hiding; are her family and animals safe?

The Summer Job

Sandra is determined to prove herself as she tries out for a summer lifesaving job – a job that will take her away from the safety of the farm into the unknown. But Sandra isn't expecting to meet someone who will change her life. She soon discovers that people can be manipulative and deceitful. Will she navigate the turbulent waters of first love and a new job.

Lavender and Pearls

Jackie and her brother Hayden are sent to stay at their eccentric aunt's antique shop in New Zealand, where they discover a magical secret. When her family members start to go missing, Jackie must venture into fantastical and dangerous new lands to save them. Will Jackie rescue her family? And what secrets will she discover along the way?

The Dramatic Bubble

Kenzie wants to focus on her school exams with no distractions, but cupid, COVID and the government have other ideas. Will the Catholic boy be a distraction for her, or the only thing that holds her together as her family life collapses?

Kaylee's Secret Mission

Still struggling from her mum's death, Kaylee is sent away from all she's ever known to move into a mansion with her father and brother she never knew. Kaylee escapes into her spy books... and then finds out that her new brother is also a sleuth fan. Together they have fun with the spy toys until she finds out their toys might be the difference between life and death. Secrets are hiding within the walls of this mansion. And Kaylee is determined to uncover them...